MERRY THANKSGIVING

By Natasha Wing
Illustrated by Isidre Mones

HarperFestival®
A Division of HarperCollins*Publishers*

To my agent and friend, Linda Pratt
—N.W.

To Nuria
—I.M.

HarperCollins®, ®, and HarperFestival are trademarks of HarperCollins Publishers Inc.
Merry Thanksgiving
Text copyright © 2005 by Natasha Wing
Illustrations copyright © 2005 by Isidre Mones
Manufactured in China by South China Printing Company Ltd.

For information address HarperCollins Children's Books,
a division of HarperCollins Publishers, 1350 Avenue of the Americas, New York, NY 10019.
www.harperchildrens.com
Library of Congress catalog card number: 2004108598
Typography by Joe Merkel
1 2 3 4 5 6 7 8 9 10
❖
First Edition

As soon as Joey learned how to write, he wrote lists to help him remember things.

He made a list of things to bring to his friend's clubhouse. He made a list of places to look for his missing socks.

Today Joey was making the most important list of all—his Christmas list.

He found a piece of paper on his mother's desk and wrote everything down.

"It's not even Thanksgiving yet," said Mrs. Melvin.

"I want to send it early so Santa doesn't forget to put everything in his sack," said Joey. "Last year he forgot the ant farm."

Mrs. Melvin told Joey that Grandma and Grandpa and his aunts and uncles and cousins would be arriving soon.

"You need to clean your room, and I need to go shopping for our Thanksgiving dinner."

"Don't forget the turkey," said Joey.

"It's on the top of my list," said Mrs. Melvin. "If only I could find it."

"Make another one," suggested Mr. Melvin.

"I'll make it!" volunteered Joey. At the top of the list he put "turkey" with two exclamation points.

"Oh, fiddlesticks. I can't remember the ingredients for Aunt Myrtle's pumpkin pie," said Mrs. Melvin. "Or Uncle Albert's stuffing."

"That's not a problem," said Mr. Melvin. "Ask the family when they get here, then go shopping."

Joey made a list of the relatives as they arrived. He put little stars next to his cousins' names.

Joey and his cousins pretended they were pilgrims. Louie was the leader because he was the tallest.

They sang karaoke.
Josie was the loudest.

Then they had a race
to see who could get to
the pizza first. Junior won.
He was the fastest.

Just when the last relative arrived, a terrible snowstorm blew in.

"What am I going to do?" said Mrs. Melvin. "I have my whole family to feed for Thanksgiving, and I can't get to the store. Now what?"

"It'll clear up," said Mr. Melvin.

But it never did.

On Thanksgiving morning, the trees were covered in snow. But worst of all, the roads were closed.

Uncle Roger looked out the window. "The only way to get through this storm is with a sleigh!"

"Santa has a sleigh," said Joey.

"Too bad he's not heading this way until Christmas Eve," said Uncle Roger.

"Thanks to Mother Nature, we're not going to have Thanksgiving dinner," Mrs. Melvin announced.

Grandma sighed. "Let's be like the pilgrims and make the best of what's here."

Joey made a list. "Well, it looks like we're having sardines, peas, beets, pearl onions, garbanzo beans, and tapioca pudding."

Mrs. Melvin burst into tears.

Joey gave her a big hug. "It's okay, Mom. Everything we need is right here."

Everyone was setting the dining room table when there was a strange noise outside.

Faintly at first, then louder and louder came the sound of sleigh bells.

"Santa Claus!" shouted Joey.

Everyone ran to the window. On the front lawn, Santa landed his reindeer.

Mrs. Melvin opened the front door.

"Am I too late?" asked Santa, stomping the snow off his boots.
"Actually, you're quite a bit early," said Mrs. Melvin.
"Did you bring everything on my list?" shouted Joey.

Santa stepped inside, opened his sack, and pulled out some butter, potatoes, rolls, stuffing mix, cranberries, and a turkey. Joey was confused. Where was the giant ant farm?

"I normally don't deliver this early, but Mrs. Claus thought this might be an emergency."

"May I see that list, Santa?" asked Mrs. Melvin. "This is my grocery list. How did you get it?"

"Joey must have sent the wrong list!" exclaimed Mr. Melvin.

"Now that we have all the ingredients, would you like to stay for Thanksgiving dinner?" asked Mrs. Melvin.

Santa grabbed his belly. "My suit could use a little filling out."

While Mr. and Mrs. Melvin baked and cooked, the cousins took turns sitting on Santa's lap and telling him what they wanted for Christmas.

Then everyone ate and ate and ate until there was no turkey left.

Santa patted his stuffed belly. "Sorry to eat
and run, but I have someplace I need to be."
"Don't forget my list!" called Joey.

Santa winked and off he flew, chuckling,
"Ho, ho, ho! Merry Thanksgiving!"